MANTEE

For Half-Pint

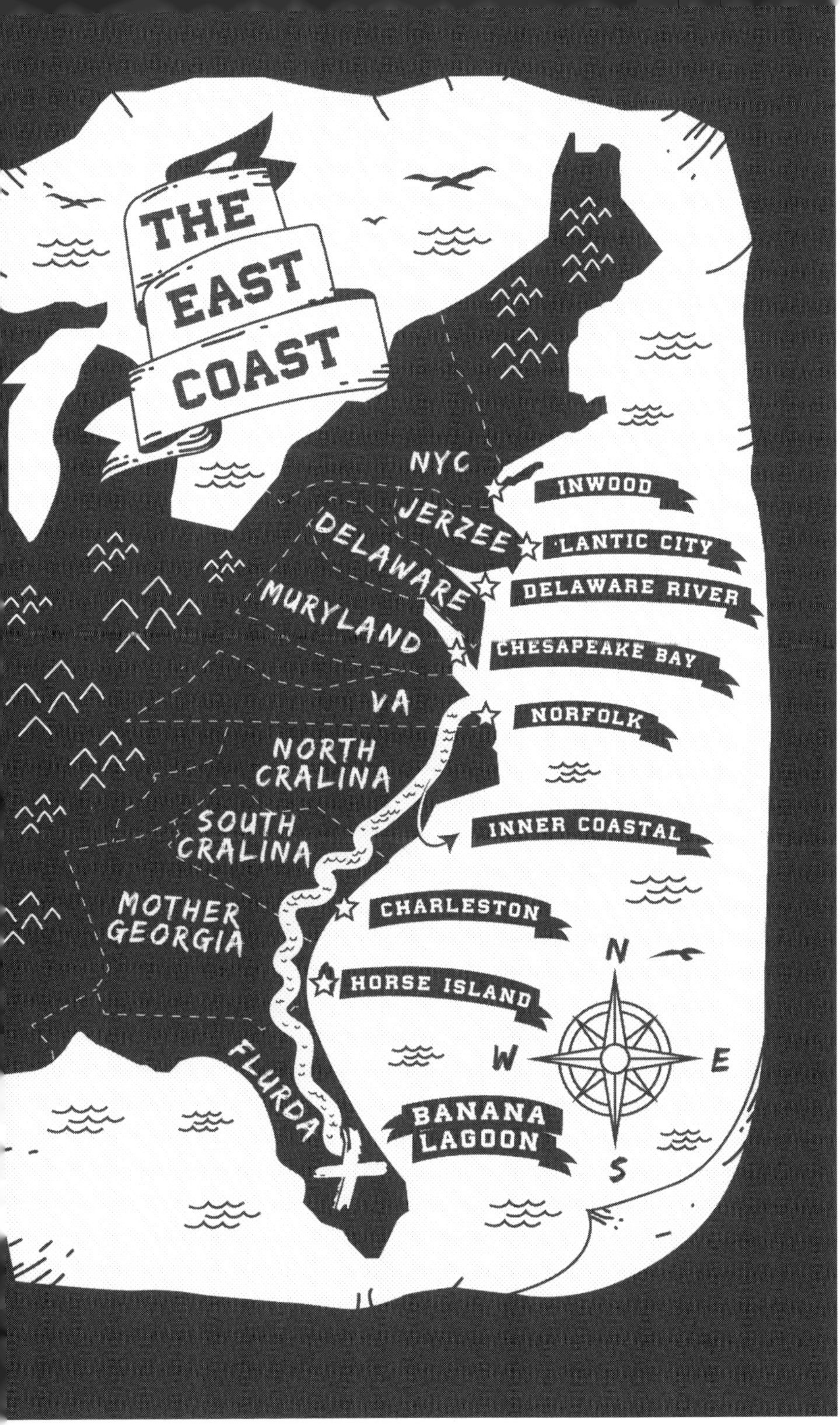
THE EAST COAST
NYC
INWOOD
JERZEE
'LANTIC CITY
DELAWARE
DELAWARE RIVER
MURYLAND
CHESAPEAKE BAY
VA
NORFOLK
NORTH CRALINA
INNER COASTAL
SOUTH CRALINA
CHARLESTON
MOTHER GEORGIA
HORSE ISLAND
FLURDA
BANANA LAGOON
N
W
E
S

CHAPTER 1

NYC

I CAN'T EXPLAIN IT, I'm just excited by life.

I live in Manhattan, maybe you've heard of it? Lots of people live here; artists, construction workers, and many others earning a living day in and day out. People visit the city just to be close to the energy.

The weather is hot in the summer and cold as a brick in the winter, but I don't mind. When it snows and the city shuts down, it's paradise. I once skied from Union Square to Rockefeller Center after a blizzard; thirty-five blocks on a pair of junky skis I found in the trash, but it was magical.

I ride my bike all over the city. Across the Brooklyn Bridge, through the bramble in Central Park, racing cars in the midtown tunnel, I don't care that it's dangerous. Manhattan is like one big great playground.

The neighborhood where I live is called Inwood. It's way uptown. I live in a six-story walk-up with a bunch of cousins I barely know. There are never any adults around. My room is the size of a closet, but that's okay. I'm not home much anyway, I need to be outdoors, always.

I live right by the water where the Harlem River flows. There are so many boats here; tankers, barges, cruisers, anything that can float is out on the water. In the river there are plenty of fish too; porgies, fluke, even sea bass. The fish are too grimy to eat, but they love being around that New York energy and I love to watch 'em swim.

My favorite place to spot fish is the ol' dock. The ol' dock is what's left of an abandoned boatyard. It looks like something you'd see in a swamp; there's even a broken-down shack on top. The ol' dock must've been mighty in ancient times, launching ships to sea, but now it's a wooden relic, slowly sinking into the river. Manhattan is full of surprises.

Last year I bought a small inflatable boat to get closer to the fish. It's blue with white stripes just like the Yanks, so I named it the *Bronx Bomber*. Every morning I go down to the ol' dock and blow up the *Bomber*. It takes about an hour to inflate and I huff and puff til I'm tired as a dog, but it's worth it when the *Bomber* takes shape. I love pushing off the ol' dock and gliding out into the water.

One thing to know about the Harlem River is that it's fast. The first time I set sail, the tide almost swept me out to sea. I had to jump overboard and swim back to shore, pulling the *Bomber* behind me. I've gotten a lot smarter since then. Now, I sail with the tides, upstream when they come in, downstream when they go out. I use my arms as oars. I paddle first on one side, then the other, zigzagging up the river. Sometimes, when the weather is calm, I sprinkle bread crumbs in the water til I'm surrounded by fish; I even hand-feed the bravest ones. Manhattan creatures are a special breed.

The Harlem River has changed over the years. There used to be small piers everywhere, but they've been replaced by many buildings. On some days it's impossible to find a place to tie up my boat, but that's okay, cause I know about a secret spot. A spot that's all mine: the power plant.

New York Electric & Gas built the plant years ago. It's like a giant factory and there are smokestacks all over and it stinks, so no one goes there. Regular people stay away, that is, but not me. I'm an explorer. I found my way in through a secret canal. I found a huge pipe that gushes hot water into the river. In fact, that's where I first saw tropical fish. That's where I first saw a mantee. In NYC!

CHAPTER 2

MANTEE

I LOVED Mantee ever since I first laid eyes on her pudgy gray face. She popped up out of the water and those blinking eyes and big ol' belly looked just like a sea cow. She must've known we'd be friends too, cause the first sound I heard her make was a magnificent "chuff!"

I know mantees are supposed to live in Flurda; I read about it in the NY Public Library. Mantees don't like cold water at all. If they get too chilly, that's the end of 'em, so you can imagine my surprise when I saw her floating by. I was paddling along on the river and had just discovered a way into the power plant. There was a big sign that said KEEP OUT, but do they expect me to listen? A fence blocked the opening to a narrow channel, but if I lay down flat in the *Bomber*, do you know what I could do? Float right under that nasty fence.

The channel led to a dark tunnel. It was a little scary if I'm being honest, but as I floated into the darkness, I could feel the water getting warmer. Up ahead, a giant pipe gushed into the canal. Water sprayed everywhere and I squirmed as it rained on my skin; it was hot! The *Bomber* rocked and nearly flipped, so I dove on my stomach and managed to steady the raft. The current pushed me along and I lost track of everything, but up ahead was a light. Up ahead was a secret pool.

The first thing I noticed when I floated into the pool was all the colorful fish. There was a group of bright yellow ones that passed right under my boat; I couldn't believe it. Clownfish, puffers, even weird ones that glowed. These definitely weren't NYC fish and I figured some gangster released them into the water. On the wall was a rusty sign that said DISCHARGE CANAL. I don't think anyone had been down here for years, but at least a faint bulb was giving off light. I mean, how else would I have seen Mantee? How else would my life have changed forever?

The water was cloudy and I spotted a shape moving below. My heart started pounding. I paddled closer; it was huge. The water churned and then Mantee burst above the surface in a big rolling ball of bubbles. She squawked loudly, introducing herself. I laughed back in amazement.

Mantee looks like a dolphin, just rounder and wrinkly. She rolled over and I saw a big ol' scar on her flipper. She quickly went under, then popped up next to me, exhaling with a whoosh. We studied each other closely. Water dripped from her snout, she was missing teeth. Her whiskers began to twitch, then she let out a massive sneeze, spraying my face with sticky goo. She was the cutest thing I'd ever seen and I could tell it was going to be a wonderful summer.

Over the next few months, Mantee and I learned a lot about each other. At first she was shy, but I always make sure to smile and speak in a calm voice so she knows I mean no harm. Each day when I arrive, Mantee comes to greet me. The first thing I do is lower myself into the pool and swim. She'll paddle close and then we'll float together, never touching. Then one day, it happened. Mantee rose up out of the water and put her flipper in my hand. I couldn't believe it and shook with joy. Then we drifted around the canal together, laughing; it's all we could think to do with this fantastic feeling.

Mantees are much smarter than you realize. They're also sensitive. For instance, my mood affects Mantee. If I'm buzzing with happiness, we'll swim together, but if I'm dog-tired from paddling, we'll just relax and float near the surface. Sometimes she gets really sleepy and needs to rest, so when I see those eyes get heavy, I'll leave her alone; she trusts me that way.

Mantee is always on the lookout for food and that usually means seaweed. I never tried seaweed til Mantee taught me and now we eat together all the time. We'll dive down to the bottom of the pool and pick the best bunch; it's delicious! Sometimes if seaweed's not around, I'll bring some grimy lettuce from the deli. It's not the best, but she seems to like it and we can munch for hours.

On certain days, Mantee will lay her head sideways in the water and just look at me. When this happens, I'll talk to her and tell her how much I like her. I know she doesn't really understand what I'm saying, but that's how we connect. I read in a book once about how mantees can form groups and at first this made me sad cause she's all alone, but then I realized that I'm her family. We're alike in so many ways. We're both survivors on our own in the big city.

CHAPTER 3

THE DEATH CULT

ONE THING TO know about NYC is that it's full of gangsters. You can always tell a gangster cause they stay up all night like vampires. I'm up at the crack of dawn so our paths usually never cross, but sometimes near sunset, when I'm bringing in the *Bomber* and the gangsters are crawling out of their beds, I'll see them. In fact, that's what happened this very day. I was gliding my boat to shore and there on the ol' dock stood the Death Cult.

There are lots of gangs in the city: the Mongrels, the Curs, but the worst of all is the Death Cult. True bullies, every one of 'em. They strut around NYC looking for trouble. Of course, it's just my luck they started showin' up at the riverfront.

I slowly sailed the *Bomber* into the dock, looking warily at the gangsters. Four of 'em, including the big

boss, Trik, stood waiting. I heard stories about Trik, scary
ones; but so what, I'm not afraid of anyone. I reached for
a post to tie up my rope, but Trik didn't like that one bit
and sneered.

"Who are you?"

"I'm CC."

"What are you doin' on the river?"

"Fishin'."

"Liar."

The other gangsters laughed quietly. I smiled cause
I'm a good person, but I know a shakedown when I
see one.

"I don't want any trouble," I replied.

"The dock belongs to us. You wanna use it, pay."

Trik's eyes narrowed and I knew it was for real. Here's
the thing about gangsters: they have nasty tongues and
their words hurt, but if you bow to 'em then you'll never
get back up, so let their words bounce off.

"I'm broke," I declared. I knew this would make them
frantic and sure enough, the lowlifes in the back got
jumpy. Trik grinned a mouth full of teeth.

"You tryin' to hustle us?" Trik accused. "I thought
you were nice? I saw you out in your boat and thought,
finally, here's someone who's nice, but you're just a hustler
like everyone we meet."

"Naw" I replied, pulling the *Bomber* out of the water.

I couldn't think of anything else to say, so I opened the air plugs in the hull and started deflating the boat. Wind rushed through tiny valves making a hissing noise. I could see they were getting red-faced mad. Trik flashed a knife.

"You sure you're broke?" Trik asked, running the blade along the edge of my boat. If the *Bomber* got slashed, how would I ever see Mantee? Reluctantly, I pulled out my last ten-dollar bill and asked if it was enough. "Don't worry," Trik whispered, taking the bill from my hand, "as long as you pay, everything will be alright and if you ever come back here, remember, that's the way it is."

I sighed as the gangsters disappeared back into the city. That night I took a walk down by the river and watched container ships sail by on their way out to sea. If I ever wanted to see Mantee again, I'd have to be quiet, hug the shore, always be on the lookout for trouble. So that's just what I did.

The next day I cast off from the railyard. It was tougher to lower the *Bomber* into the water from there and I cut my leg on a piling, but soon enough I was back on the river. As I sailed into the power plant, I could hear splashing in the distance and knew Mantee was active. I sailed into the secret pool and right away she started rubbing against the *Bomber*. She'd swim around in circles, rubbing it on all sides. I wasn't sure what she was expressing, but it made me happy.

"Mantee, we gotta make sure nobody pulls any stunts on us. I'm not worried about it though, cause these gangsters are empty-headed," I whispered. She agreed and we took a nice swim. That's one of the things Mantee taught me, there's no reason in the world to worry.

Over the next week, I didn't see any gangsters, so I forgot all about the Death Cult. A good thing, too, cause Mantee and I discovered water games. We started playin' a game called BULLSEYE where I'd try to splash water into her mouth. She loves this one; I can tell cause she bobs up and down and makes bubbles in the pool. Another one we'll play is MIRROR. I'll make a movement with my head and Mantee will do the same thing. It's amazing how we reflect energy back and forth, I could live moments like these forever. But of course...

...the Death Cult returned. I saw 'em when I was floating out of the power plant. I was lying flat on my back in the *Bomber*, gliding under the nasty fence, when they appeared out of nowhere, four of 'em lookin' straight down. They could try scaring me to death, but I'd never let 'em.

"You know it ain't fair," Trik moaned, yanking my boat to the shore. "You're out here having fun while we're stuck on these rocks. And we got problems you can't even imagine."

"Don't you feel bad runnin' scams?" I replied, getting out of the boat.

"I don't feel anything," Trik answered.

This made the hair on the back of my neck stand up. I was gonna make a run for it, but Trik pulled me close. "You know the deal."

"I don't know nuthin," I murmured.

Trik looked in the direction of the power plant. "Whatcha doin' in there?"

"I told ya, nuthin."

"Wrong," Trik exclaimed. Soon I was surrounded by lowlifes staring me down, but I didn't flinch. In fact, when one of 'em tried to give me a shove, I swung around and knocked the gangster back with a wild punch. There was much confusion. Then it was off to the races.

"Get 'em!" I heard them yell as I dashed toward the street. They dove at my feet, but I'm a good runner and hard to catch. Soon I was blocks away. I blazed clean through Inwood Hill Park and thought I lost 'em, but they must've called ahead, cause next thing I know, I was tackled with a swift hit. It knocked the wind clean outta me.

The rest of the gangsters caught up and started circling. Then they pinned me to the ground. Trik straddled my chest, which was pounding. "I'm gonna do you a favor and make this quick, cause you're small and not at all important."

"Get outta here," I replied. This didn't go over well and Trik started pounding me hard. Somebody kicked me in the ribs. They probably woulda kept going, but thunder rumbled in the distance and it started to drizzle. That's another thing to know about gangsters, they hate gettin' wet.

"Let's go," one of 'em shouted.

Trik paused and looked up at the clouds. I was nervous and shaking. "You oughta go home," Trik whispered, before punching me one last time. The world spun and went blurry.

I woke up later in a vacant lot. It was quiet. Too quiet for the city. Usually there are car horns and jackhammers pounding away, but it was nighttime and everyone must've been asleep. I sat up and let the rain drizzle on my face. I needed a moment to gather my thoughts so I took a deep breath. I was hungry and thirsty, but if I can survive the Death Cult, I can survive anything. A look of determination was on my face and I vowed to protect Mantee at all costs as the moon rose above NYC.

CHAPTER 4

THE STORM

IT WAS ALMOST the first full moon of August. Comin' so early in the month, I knew there would be wild energy in the air and sure enough, I found myself in for adventure. First thing I did was start rushin' back toward the river. Usually NYC smells grimy, so you forget the sea is nearby, but tonight a wind was pickin' up and the smell of the ocean was strong. A lightning bolt cracked and lit up the sky.

The next five blocks were the longest of my life. I ran unsteady, trembling at the thought of seeing the Death Cult again, but I had to get back to Mantee, she could be in trouble. I reached the river and there was the *Bomber* still intact. I started scramblin' down the bank, but looked up at the sky and paused; scary lookin' clouds were rollin' in. The temp was dropping and I knew a big one was gonna hit. I jumped into the *Bomber* and set off just as the skies opened up with rain. Torrents of it started comin' down and by the time I reached the power plant, I was drenched to the skin. As I floated into the dark tunnel, I could see Death Cult graffiti on the walls and hear shouting in the distance. I knew in my bones somethin' was wrong.

I paddled quickly. My bummy eyes had trouble adjusting in the dark, but that's okay cause my other senses sharpened. I entered the secret pool and saw light from the dim bulb bouncing off the gangsters' faces, makin' 'em look possessed. I thought maybe I caught 'em by surprise, but no such luck.

"Never thought we'd see you again," shouted Trik, standing on a ledge above the water.

"What are you doin'?" I responded.

"Nuthin' nice!"

My stomach clenched when I saw what they were up to. A bunch of Death Cult lowlifes had ropes tied around Mantee. One was wrapped around her big ol' belly and another was wound tight around her tail. She squirmed and squealed as they tried pulling her to the side of the pool.

"Stop, you're hurtin' her!" I yelled.

"What is this thing?" Trik shouted back.

"It's a mantee."

"A what?"

"A mantee."

"Ain't no matter, we're takin' it."

"You can't!' I replied.

"Then we're killin' it."

Once Trik said those words, I started seein' red. That's never happened before and somehow I became a different person. I found myself climbing out of the water and running to a place called JUNCTION ROOM. Lights from control panels flickered and there were knobs and gauges all over, so I just started turning everything in sight. I was really goin' off. I turned a giant valve that said PRESSURE PUMP and soon all the pipes started shaking. I guess the strain was too much, cause there was a giant explosion and water started bursting from the ceiling. You know, there are many things in life I can't explain, but somehow the gangsters got washed away in a flood that night. I howled like a dog when I saw 'em get flushed down the canal. The water was knee deep, but that didn't stop me from runnin' back to the pool and divin' right in.

I swam straight to Mantee. Seeing her up close made the anger fade and brought me back to myself. I put my hand under Mantee's chin and she nestled her head in my arms. I could feel a warm glow deep inside me, I don't know how else to describe it.

"Do you trust me?" I whispered.

Mantee moved slightly in my arms and nibbled my fingers with her teeth. There was a sweetness in her eyes and I knew the answer was yes.

"Then we gotta get you outta here. C'mon."

At first, Mantee didn't want to leave and I don't blame her. I don't know if she'd ever been outside? I climbed into my raft and gave her rope a tug, but she wouldn't budge. I thought for a moment, then I put my finger in the water right above her head and made tiny circles on the surface. That got her attention and each time I did it, she'd move a tiny bit forward. That's how we got out of the power plant and into the Harlem River.

The current in the river was rippin' like I'd never seen. Instead of calming down, the storm had gotten worse. The wind was so strong, it didn't just blow water on the river, it flung it up into my face. I leaned forward in the *Bomber* and held onto Mantee for dear life. The two of us began shootin' downstream.

The Harlem River flows into the East River, which separates Manhattan from Brooklyn. Normally I love seein' skyscrapers at night from this spot, but the spray from the river raked my face and I lost visibility. All I could see were the rough edges of the Empire State Building as lightning flashed in the sky.

We were moving extremely fast now. The East River

empties into New York Harbor, which was convulsin' with waves; I saw a big one crash into Lady Liberty. Truth be told, it was a scary sight, but I'm a tough person and that means I stay calm when things get dangerous.

"Mantee," I pleaded, "stay with me."

I wrapped the rope tight around my forearm and braced for a bumpy ride. The cord cut my skin and burned somethin' fierce as we started reelin' out to sea. I think I saw a strip of land in Jerzee, but after that, it was all open ocean. The rolling of the sea was heavy and covered in great patches of foam. The *Bomber* started movin' up and down waves like a roller coaster, the swells were so big. That put the fear of God in me and I started feelin' sick; I couldn't tell where the sky stopped and the ocean began. A barrel of water rose up and suddenly the *Bomber* was pointin' straight to the heavens. I could feel myself fallin' through the air and I thought I was going to die the very next moment.

But I didn't die.

CHAPTER 5

'LANTIC CITY

I WOKE up on an empty beach. It was daytime and the light blinded my eyes. I squinted and tried to sit up but was too weary. My shoes were gone, they must've been blown clean off. I tried to piece together the events from last night, but it all had the unreal quality of a dream. I could remember gangsters. A flood. Mantee.

Mantee?

I struggled and pushed myself off the ground. What happened to her? I stumbled forward toward the water. The sea was peaceful now and waves lapped gently on the sand. Two sharp rocks jutted out of the surf and on top was the *Bomber*, torn to pieces. I thought I would feel awful and sad seeing my boat ripped up, but I was just happy to be alive. I took the raft in my arms and sighed.

I was standing at the edge of a small cove that divided

the land and sea. The tide was low and clear except for a gray shape movin' through the water. I remained still, not daring to breathe. It was Mantee, swimmin' not more than twenty yards away.

"Mantee," I sputtered, forcing myself into action. I splashed into the water and soon I was up to my chest. It was only a short distance to swim but I could barely do it, my arms were so tired. I had to work my legs like pistons to stay afloat, but that did the trick. I reached Mantee and gave her the biggest hug. She could've let me die in that ocean, but she didn't. I don't know why Mantee cares about me, but she does.

"Thank God you're alive," I exclaimed. Mantee snorted in response, but her head was low and I could see somethin' was wrong.

"What's the matter?" I asked. Treading water, I looked down and saw the rope still coiled around her big ol' belly. There was blood under one flipper and I knew I had to get the cord off quick. Without thinking I took a deep breath and dove straight down. I swam directly under Mantee and tried desperately to get the line off, but all that time in the water had tightened the knot. No matter what I did, it wouldn't come undone. It felt impossible, but I'm not one to give up easy, so I kept workin' til my fingers trembled and Mantee was finally free.

"Ay yo!" I shouted, exploding to the surface. Mantee raised her head and chirped like a bird, happy to be set loose. For the next few hours we drifted around and talked til it felt like we were the only creatures in the world. It was so peaceful and the water was warm as a bath.

"How do you find these places?" I asked Mantee in amazement. Mantee barked in response, then nuzzled my neck and dove down to feed on seagrass. Watching Mantee eat made me realize how hungry I'd become, so I told her, "Wait for me here." Then I headed to shore and made my way to the top of a nearby sand dune. From there I could see for miles and what a sight! Giant casinos gleamed in the distance and I knew this must be 'Lantic City.

Broke and starving, I set off for town. One thing to know about life, if you ever need money fast, washing dishes is the way. Check in the alleys behind restaurants, that's where the workers hang out. Sure enough, I soon found some cooks playing cards behind one of the casinos. Now, I'm not shy, I'm the type to walk right up to a person and say, " I'm CC Woods and I'm lookin' for work," so that's just what I did. The crew stopped their game and studied me close. I must've looked grimy after all the things I'd been through, but there was one cook named Sunny that just shrugged and asked, "You wash dishes?"

"Yeah," I replied.

"Alright, here you go." Sunny tossed a dish towel in my direction. I figured if I didn't make money then Mantee and I were goners, so I caught it with determination and in the backdoor I went.

The restaurant was called CITY BISTRO and it was bustlin', so I rolled up my sleeves, marched right up to that hot, steamy sink and dove in. I scrubbed dishes, pots, forks, glasses, you name it. It was an enormous job and I worked well into the night, but at the end, when the last plate was cleaned, the crew gave me slaps on the back and fifty bucks. "Look at you now!" they laughed.

"You did alright," Sunny grinned.

"Thanks," I replied.

"You eat yet?" Sunny asked.

"Naw." I answered.

"C'mon."

Sunny only lived a few blocks from the casinos, but in that neighborhood, it was all crumblin' homes and empty lots. In fact, Sunny's place looked like a wooden relic, but inside was warm and bright with carpet and everything. Sunny had lots of groceries and cooked up a tremendous dinner. I was like a starvin' dog the way I ate so fast, but Sunny didn't mind and just smiled.

"Hungry, huh?"

"It's good," I mumbled with a mouthful. I proceeded to clean my entire plate, then worked up the courage to ask, "Could I borrow some lettuce for a friend?"

Sunny laughed, "Yeah, you can borrow some lettuce for a friend."

I don't know why, but Sunny and I got along. We joked around for a while after dinner, then said our goodbyes and I made my way back to the cove. Mantee was still rootin' around for seaweed, so I swam out and delivered the bundle of lettuce. Mantee whistled with excitement and devoured it with big messy chomps. "Hungry, huh?" I asked. Mantee grunted in response, then dove back down.

It was still hot out, so I swam to shore and decided to sleep on the beach. The stars were out and light from the casinos reflected off the ocean as I snoozed away.

For the next week, Mantee foraged for food and I washed dishes non-stop. Each day I made fifty bucks, just enough to buy lunch and I'd bank the rest. Our evenings were spent floatin' around the cove. It was nice here in 'Lantic City, but I couldn't help thinking about the approaching fall weather. It was a big problem. Deep in my heart I knew Mantee couldn't go back to NYC, too many gangsters. She couldn't stay in Jerzee either, it was mid-August and soon to be freezin'. So I made a big decision then and there, I had to get Mantee to Flurda, whatever it took.

Have you ever had such a crazy idea that you got up early in the morning, ran to your job and felt magnificent? That was me. If somethin' spilled in the kitchen that day, I was on it with a bucket and broom. I tried to keep my plan a secret from the crew at CITY BISTRO, but some things are too big to keep inside. I had to tell someone, so after closing time, I brought Sunny back to the cove to see Mantee. Sunny stared in surprise.

"What is it?" Sunny asked.

"It's a mantee," I replied.

"What are you gonna do with it?"

"I gotta get her to Flurda."

"How in the world you gonna do that?" Sunny asked.

"If I had a small boat, she'd follow me. I know she would."

Sunny thought for a moment, then nodded and told me about the fishin' docks across town. I went there straight away and was introduced to a salty ol' sailor who worked on boats. I told the Ol' Salt I was plannin' on sailin' to Flurda and didn't have much cash. The Ol' Salt smirked and led me to a tiny rowboat with an ancient engine in the back. It was a real rust bucket, but I loved it; bought it on the spot.

Then I took a deep breath.

With that, I knew our days in 'Lantic City were comin' to an end. I worked a few more shifts to make extra cash, then hung up the dish towel for good. The night before I left was unforgettable. There was a party at Sunny's house with a big spread of cake and drinks. Everyone was happy and I was in awe. Listenin' to the music and voices had me so lost in the moment that I didn't hear Sunny at first.

"...I can't believe you're actually gonna do it. I'll miss ya, you know."

"I can't believe it either," I replied and gave Sunny a big hug.

The next morning while everyone slept, I made my way down to the docks and loaded up the rust bucket with supplies and extra containers of gas. The Ol' Salt was there and looked worried, so I tried to be reassuring.

"I'll be alright," I said.

"Stay outta the ocean in this thing, it won't last," the Ol' Salt warned.

"You got it."

"The first river you'll come to is the Delaware," the Ol' Salt continued, "but keep goin' til you get to the Chesapeake. Make for the inner waters down there."

"I will," I replied.

I started the engine and it sputtered to life. As I

shoved off into the calm channel, I waved goodbye to the Ol' Salt. The motor was chuggin' steady, so I decided to name my new boat *Lil' Putt Putt*. I took a deep breath of salty air and threaded my way past rocks and reefs til I reached the cove and Mantee.

I'm always thrilled when I see her movin' through the water and this time was no different. In fact, I was so eager to show off, I drove *Lil' Putt Putt* directly toward Mantee, but she panicked and I quickly learned not to do that. Poor Mantee was scared of the boat, so I killed the engine and just floated in the general area. If there's one thing that Mantee has taught me, it's patience; I have to go slow and build her trust. Gradually, Mantee became curious and swam around *Lil' Putt Putt*. I fed her lettuce off the side and she rubbed against the metal hull. I soon learned the best thing was to steer parallel to Mantee. I'd move about twenty feet away, then make circles in the water with an oar, calling her over. This back and forth continued til we made it out of the cove and I knew Mantee was stickin' with me for good.

I'll always wonder what might've happened if we went back to NYC, but I'll settle for lettin' it be a mystery. Mantee and I motored into the big blue sea with a spankin' breeze blowin' south.

Chapter 6

Zarks

It was a golden morning as we cruised down the coast. Sun sparkled on the water and we sailed with the ocean current. Mantee began the day swimmin' next to *Lil' Putt Putt* and we made good progress, but as the day wore on, she disappeared into the sea. At first I didn't think anything of it, but as the hours ticked by, I became a nervous wreck. Where'd she go?

"Mantee?!" I yelled in all directions.

I almost gave up hope of seein' her again, but then she popped up next to *Lil' Putt Putt* and squawked like a bird. I was so thrilled, I immediately gave her a bundle of lettuce as a reward. She swam off and returned four times that day and I realized that's how it would be on this trip, I was her escort. She had missions in the big ocean and it was my job to keep us movin' in the right direction.

That night, we made camp in a marshy inlet. There was solid ground there, so that was good enough for me. I anchored *Lil' Putt Putt* in shallow water and watched Mantee vacuum up seagrass under the boat. I was desperately hungry myself and waded ashore. Right up on the beach was a cluster of oysters and I grinned at my good luck. I hardly ever get to eat real, fresh oysters and I do love the lil' things. I gathered 'em by the armful and scarfed down the insides of many shells. After fillin' my belly, I built a roarin' fire right on the sand. I was so content, I didn't even notice when a cloud of insects appeared. Nasty mosquitoes on the hunt, so I got a blanket from the boat and lay down for bed. The echoes of some far-off lighthouse had me relaxed, but I didn't sleep well. Thoughts of beginning a long journey that could bring all sorts of dangers kept me awake.

The next morning, a heavy fog rolled over the sea, making it disappear into the sky. I wasn't sure if we should leave, but after studyin' the morning light, I guessed it would soon burn off, so away we went into the mist. At first I couldn't see anything, it was like movin' through a tunnel of clouds, but as long as I could hear the crashin' surf, I knew we were close to shore. By noon the fog started thinning, then suddenly the sun broke through and there appeared a giant container ship. Its hull grew steadily larger as it bore down on us.

"Watch where you're goin'!" I shouted, swingin' *Lil'
Putt Putt* hard to the side. Mantee and I just made it out
of the way as the boat powered by, creating an enormous
wake. The trailing waves hit *Lil' Putt Putt* and each time
one struck, I seemed to hang in the air before slammin'
back down. Eventually I righted the craft and got my
bearings. Many ships were comin' and goin', some
blasting their horns and I knew this must be the
Delaware River the Ol' Salt told me about. It was much
wider than I thought and busy with traffic, so we had to
dodge many vessels. I began to get nervous for Mantee. If
she got struck by one of these lunatics, she'd be done for.
I tried to chart a course through the mayhem and keep
Mantee close, but it was tricky. A speedboat started
bankin' toward us and I knew it was gonna be trouble.

"Mantee, look out," I exclaimed with anxiety in my
voice. Wavin' my hands I yelled, "Hey, you're gonna run
us down!" The driver looked half asleep as the vessel
swept by, narrowly missing Mantee.

"You coulda killed us!" I shouted back at 'em.

The situation was serious as we bobbed and weaved til
we finally sailed outta the fray. My heart was still
pounding when we made it to the other side. It was at
that moment somethin' clicked in my mind and I realized
that a big danger to Mantee would be boats. She always
swims so close to the surface and doesn't have a care in

the world, even *Lil' Putt Putt* could hurt her. This made me uncertain. How could I get her safely down the coast with all these maniacs and their ships? "Gotta be alert," I whispered to myself. That was the price of Mantee's safety and nothing could distract my attention or an accident would occur.

For the next few days we plowed through the waters off Delaware (or was it Muryland)? At night we'd stop at some strip of sand and I'd get what sleep I could. All the while, the Ol' Salt's words echoed in my ears, "Stay outta the ocean in this thing, it won't last." It was like an omen that made the trip seem doomed. There's no doubt I try to be brave and meet danger head on, but I couldn't quite shake a fear about what lurks in the ocean. Soon enough, I spotted a zark.

We had just passed a lighthouse and the mouth of a giant bay opened before us, it must've been the Chesapeake. That's when the silver-gray fin appeared and I knew right away it was a zark. A six-footer by the looks of it. The fierce creature was dashing this way and that, lookin' for dinner.

"Get you - get!" I shouted, but it didn't listen. Then I caught sight of several more. I took a deep breath and understood this was the time for action if I wanted to help Mantee. Quickly I reached into my stash of supplies and grabbed a sharp knife.

"Manteelookoutbehindyou!" I screamed, slurring my words. One of the zarks was headin' straight for her belly, so I jumped into the water like a wild animal and brought the knife down hard into its head. At first it didn't seem to do much damage, but the water began turnin' red and I knew the hit was true.

Another zark rushed under Mantee, turning over while opening its mouth full of nasty teeth. I think Mantee tried to roll sideways and knock it away, but all the splashin' blocked my view, so I took a lungful of air and dove down.

Have you ever seen something fight for survival? It's a scary sight and I couldn't believe the frenzy underwater. Immediately the zark lunged at me with a snap of its tail. Out of instinct, I raised the knife to protect myself. I don't know exactly what happened next, but I could feel the point catch under its mouth. The zark started thrashin' and my reflexes told me to push the knife, hard. The blade twisted and then the zark spun wildly before sinkin' down out of sight. Did I get it? Who knows. I desperately needed air and burst to the surface, expecting to be attacked any second, but the bites never came.

I struggled back into the boat and gaped at the commotion taking place where the zark I wounded had been floatin'. It was a free-for-all with cannibal zarks feedin' on their own kind. The meat must've tasted good cause they seemed to forget about us.

"C'mon Mantee," I yelled, gunnin' the motor to the limit. Off we raced across the waters of the Chesapeake. The bay was huge and I was nervous we'd be caught by the zarks and have to fight again. In fact, I never saw Mantee swim so fast. She's usually a slow grazer, but those zarks put the fear of God in us both. The crossing was long and difficult and the boat propeller almost clipped Mantee twice, but we finally made it to the other side. I ran *Lil' Putt Putt* onto a sandbar and jumped into the water with relief.

"Are you okay?" I cried out to Mantee. It was like she understood what I was sayin' cause she rolled on her back and looked at me upside down; there wasn't a scratch on her. It takes a lot of trust to be so vulnerable in front of someone and I got teary-eyed. "You don't know when to quit, do you?" I asked. Mantee huffed and I knew the answer was no.

In a rush of emotion, I stumbled out of the water and fell onto the sand. I could hear someone roarin' at the top of their lungs and realized it was me. I was so happy that Mantee was safe and I was on solid ground. "Ay yo!" I howled and my whole body was buzzin', it felt great.

CHAPTER 7

INNER COASTAL

THAT'S how they found me on the beach in VA. While I was rollin' around and screamin' the sand had filled with people. Droves of 'em, so I piped down and scanned their faces. Some were laughin', some looked surprised. I felt myself blushin' and said sorry for being wild, then turned to leave when one face stuck out from the crowd - it belonged to a person they called Shiloh and as we sized each other up I couldn't think of anything to say except, "Hi."

"You need help?" Shiloh asked

"I'm good," I replied.

"You're bleedin', you know?"

"Just scratches," I shrugged.

"We're from a church down the beach. If you wanna get fixed up and some food, it's no problem."

"I don't know," I responded. Casting a glance toward the water, I could see Mantee rootin' around for seaweed; she'd be down there for hours, knowin' her. I tried to sit up but pain shot through my body. "Did you say food?" I asked.

"Yeah," Shiloh nodded with a grin. A group of 'em helped me off the ground and we marched up the beach like a gang. Shiloh was the leader and nodded to everyone, saying things like, "Hey," "What's good?" and "Let's get it."

The whole group lived together behind an old church. When we arrived, there were teenagers everywhere and people sleepin' on extra mattresses. "It's like a halfway house, I guess," Shiloh explained. When they finally showed me the kitchen, you shoulda seen all the food I ate: beans, spaghetti, everything!

"You need a place to rest?" Shiloh asked.

"I'm dead tired," I answered with a yawn. No sooner had I said those words than I was shown a bed and fell asleep at once. That night I dreamed Mantee and I were in a lagoon and I whispered, "See all those birds, waves, and rocks, they're all yours." Mantee could speak in my dream and replied, "Lessgo," so off we swam into the sea, not worryin' about a thing.

I woke up the next morning to a song playing on church bells.

"What time is it?" I mumbled.

"Time for morning service," Shiloh answered, dressed up in a fancy outfit. "You should come, it'll help you."

The church was called DESTINY BY THE SEA and I shuffled in with the rest of the crew.

"Bless you," the preacher whispered, rubbin' water on my forehead. I liked this church straight away cause I could tell that it kept people from turnin' into gangsters. All afternoon they preached and I learned many things about life: don't gossip, don't ditch out on your friends, and most important, how to pray.

"Please God, help me get Mantee to Flurda," I whispered over and over.

After the last sermon, Shiloh declared, "I'm with you Jesus, always," and we all spilled out onto the beach. Once outside, I set off for *Lil' Putt Putt* and the gang followed along. Weaving between sunbathers and surfboards, we finally found the boat and it looked like a wreck, so they helped me drag it off the sand and into a nearby cove. The whole gang shook their heads when they heard how I expected to reach distant Flurda in such a rugged craft.

"It'll be tough to get there," Shiloh explained, "but not if you take the Inner Coastal."

"Huh?" I responded.

That's when Shiloh told me about sailin' down south.

"The east coast is a string of bays, connected by creeks and channels," Shiloh explained. "If you follow the channel markers with yellow triangles on 'em, you can get all the way from VA to Flurda and never go in the ocean. It's called sailin' the Inner Coastal."

"Wow," I replied with eyes wide open, it's all I could think to say. After the crew left, I swam out to Mantee. When Mantee saw me, she dove down to the bottom and did a slow somersault, slapping my feet with her tail. I laughed and the warm water felt like a miracle cause for the first time since our trip started, it seemed possible. If we could stay out of that nasty ocean, we just might make it.

The afternoon sun was setting but the air was still warm, so I decided to sleep on the beach. I floated out near Mantee to say goodnight and noticed she was surfacing a lot; I think that meant the seaweed was gone.

"We'll find more soon," I promised and knew we had to keep movin'. Mantee squeaked and opened her mouth, so I splashed in some water and we played a game of BULLSEYE. Then I blew a stream of bubbles under Mantee's chin. Mantee responded by diving down and sending rings of fizz up my back. It was the perfect ending to our last day in this special place.

When the sun rose in the morning, I found Shiloh and we talked a lot, mostly about places I never knew

existed. "Norfolk," Shiloh explained. "Cape Fear."
"Myrtle Beach." I couldn't remember all the names, but it
didn't matter; we never shut up for hours and it was great.
The crew knew I was movin' on and gave me a survival
kit full of water bottles, blankets, pocket knives, stuff like
that and right on top was a medal of St. Christopher.

"I'll pay you back for everything," I tried to reassure
'em.

"No way," Shiloh replied and they gave me hugs til I
was all smiles. It's hard to leave people when you're on
good terms, but Mantee and I had to keep ahead of the
weather, so our new start was made.

We puttered outta the cove with a southwest breeze.
Soon enough we sailed past the big wharves at Norfolk.
That's when I spotted a channel marker with a yellow
triangle, just like Shiloh said. We followed the yellow
markers into a broad river and soon joined a parade of
boats. I started gettin' nervous cause I knew these ships
meant trouble for Mantee. I looked over the stern and
could see her large shape beneath the surface. It had to be
tricky down there with the noise of all the propellers and
Mantee must've agreed cause she lifted her head out of
the water and let out a dramatic honk.

"Be careful Mantee," I whispered under my breath.
Despite the traffic, no one seemed to notice us, they were
too busy yelling as all the boats drew closer together. One

ship passed us pulling a barge and I could hear the
captain yelling to someone on their radio, "This is the
motorboat *Annapolis* on your bow side. Stay back you
rats! Keep your distance!"

I tried to steer clear of these maniacs but the current
kept pushin' us into the fray. Boats were passin'
constantly and I could hear chatter on radios everywhere.

"Take the VA cut down to North Cralina…"

"Watch out for logs in the Dismal Swamp…"

"Back off," I yelled as ships bore down on us, "you're
gettin' too close," but they didn't listen. Anyone with a
brain could see Mantee was about to get banged and I
started feelin' fire in my blood but had to keep calm
cause that's what survivors do. The water was churnin'
and I couldn't see below the surface so I threaded our
way through the minefield til we finally reached the
safety of a sheltered canal. Mantee came up for air right
as we slipped through the entrance to an enclosed pool. I
didn't know it then, but we had entered a canal lock.
Towering walls blocked our way and as gates swung shut
behind us, I knew we were in trouble. Water began
floodin' the basin as a lockkeeper appeared on the ledge
above us.

"What is this place?" I yelled.

"It's a lock," shouted the lockkeeper.

"A what?!"

"A lock! Fills up with water! Raises you to a high part of the river!"

"Turn it off!" I shouted.

"Can't," the lockkeeper yelled back.

Mantee started panicking and I didn't blame her, the rising water looked like it was boiling. I suddenly became dismayed with how difficult this journey was and felt like quitting. I covered my eyes with my fists but that's when Mantee got turbo-charged, rose up out of the water and almost climbed into my boat.

"Mantee?!" I sputtered, losing my balance and falling headfirst into the spray. I hit the water like a board and felt the wind go out of me. When I resurfaced, the vapor was thick and I had to blink non-stop. I couldn't see Mantee so I dove back down and there she was, floating limp underwater. This nasty lock had taken us by surprise and now we were trapped. I reached out for Mantee and somehow we found each other, then it was like everything went quiet and slowed down. I even had time to think. Why was I afraid? Mantee opened her eyes and touched my fingers to her muzzle. We hung that way til the gates lifted and we surged forward to the upstream side of the lock.

I came up for fresh air and gasped with relief. It took a while, but Mantee slowly recovered and was soon back to her old self. As we drifted down new canals, branches hung over the river and Mantee popped out of the water, eating leaves right off the trees. I smiled and confidence spread back over my body. I realized that we were lucky to be alive. I guess that's why I leaned overboard and dangled my hand in the water for no reason other than it felt good.

CHAPTER 8

BELIEVE IN THE IMPOSSIBLE

As we passed through the wilderness I became intensely interested in *Lil' Putt Putt's* motor. I'd watch it pulsate for hours and think about how to make it safe for Mantee. Soon enough, I discovered fish traps by the riverbank and bent them into wire cages that could surround the propeller. This way, if Mantee hit the blades, she'd be okay. What started as a success, though, faded when I saw scars on her back, but I didn't look at those for long, I just made a promise: Mantee, I'll protect you for days, weeks, months, years.

Now it's a whole new day. In fact, it's a whole new situation cause that afternoon I caught two fish. Not grimy ones either, but real prizes. I cooked 'em over a fire and lemme tell you, these VA fish have the best flavor, even better than a NY frank. Later when the stars appeared I started talkin' to Mantee, sayin' things like, "I gotta tell you about this Flurda place, you won't believe it" - til I was sleepy and lookin' at channel markers bobbin' in the dark. Far off in the distance an animal howled and that's the last thing I remember before falling asleep.

The next morning we cruised in gloomy weather. Mantee swam without a care in the world, but at noon it started gettin' dark and I began to feel nervous. My hair blew in the wind as I took in signs of approaching trouble. At midday I ate while still motorin' along cause I didn't like the look of the clouds in the sky. Meanwhile, a thick fog seemed to gather round us. As we cut across a wide stretch of water that was tumblin' in the wind I could feel in my bones we'd entered a dangerous bay.

Thunder boomed. Squinting at the horizon, I could see a line of rain rushing toward us and knew we were in for another squall. Crouching down in the boat with clenched teeth, I prepared myself to survive. The first wave struck *Lil' Putt Putt* with a crash. The boat surged forward and almost completely flipped before I righted the craft, but the force of the waves had dragged us over a bed of hidden rocks. The engine scraped across the bottom and without warning, ripped clean off.

I couldn't believe it and clutched the sides of *Lil' Putt Putt* as water rushed in through a gaping hole. I feared the boat was goin' down and scrambled to grab what I could, when in the blink of an eye, *Lil' Putt Putt* disappeared beneath the surface and I was in for another plunge. Now the real work began. I fought mightily to stay afloat. The strain was unbelievable and I almost drowned, but in a mad swirl of water, I felt hands grasp my shoulders and I was yanked upwards.

"I'm alive!" I yelled to my rescuers as they hauled me onto a ship in the shrieking wind. My memory is spotty about what happened next, but I must've been more tired than I thought cause before I could introduce myself, I fell fast asleep. When I woke up sometime later, the storm was over and sun shone brightly on a new day.

"You good?" I heard a voice ask.

"Not really," I murmured, trying to focus my eyes. A shadow passed over my face and I could see a group of people.

"You're lucky we came along," said a person in a tropical get-up. "I'm the Cap'n, but don't try to remember that, you just woke up."

"Where am I?" I asked.

"You're on *Lady Luck*. It's not the fastest ship around, but it's something special. You'll see."

I nodded as the Cap'n took my hand and soon I was on a tour of the most luxurious boat I'd ever seen. There were three levels and it had everything you could think of: bookshelves, dining tables, leather chairs, even a place called a STATE ROOM. Along the way I met people named Slim, Junior, Tully, and Half-Pint. I really had no idea what to say and just nodded along til we went outside and leaned against a brass rail that surrounded the hull. The Cap'n asked, "Where you headed?"

"Flurda," I answered.

"We're sailin' to South Cralina. I can take you as far as Myrtle Beach if you're willing to work and make a buck for yourself," the Cap'n proposed.

"That's good enough for me," I replied.

"Good, good," the Cap'n declared before disappearing below deck. I looked out across the helm with an empty stare. Where was Mantee?! The question jolted me awake, so I rushed to the rear of the vessel and watched riverbanks drift by, but no Mantee. A small sailboat was tied up behind *Lady Luck*, so without thinking, I shimmied out across the line and dropped onto the tiny craft. I remember the next moment like it was yesterday, cause sittin' in the cockpit was the one they called Half-Pint, a young'un of no more than six who took one look at me and asked, "Whatcha doing?"

"Lookin' for a friend," I replied.

"What for?"

"Cause she's lost."

"Can I help?"

"Yeah," I nodded, so we lay flat on our stomachs and leaned over the sides of the sailboat, tapping the water with our fingers.

"Mantee?!" I called out.

"Mantee?!" echoed Half-Pint.

"Mantee Mantee," I yelled.

"Mantee Mantee," echoed Half-Pint. The kid's eyes shined with delight at this silly game, but the whole thing frightened me and I went to bed that night with a sense of dread that Mantee was lost forever. I lay awake for hours and time seemed to drag on. I felt frustration turn to anger, but before that happened, my eyes grew heavy and closed.

The next morning my job workin' for the Cap'n began. I did all manner of work you could do on a boat: washing the deck, cleaning the galley, even scrubbin' out the toilets. The work was dirty and hard, but that's alright cause once my shift ended I was back on the tiny sailboat with Half-Pint, scanning the Inner Coastal for signs of Mantee. For days on end we searched, calling to her day and night. Many heads popped out of the water behind *Lady Luck*: turtles, stingrays, even dolphins, but no Mantee. She never came. The world seemed sad and my eyes filled with tears cause I realized my only chance now was prayin' to God for hope. Each night waves lapped against the bow and the engine throbbed til one morning, the propeller went quiet. I blinked awake to Half-Pint tapping me on the shoulder, "I seen Mantee."

"What?" I stammered. Then it hit me and I sprinted out of the cabin and jumped off the back shouting, "Ay yo!" Seconds later I hit the water and shot to the surface. There she was, the sweet creature that gives this book its name.

"Mantee," I gasped, "where you been?"

Mantee looked up from seaweed munching and gave a grunt. Then she swam round and round and kept watching me, like I was being sized up. Finally, her muzzle twitched, her snout opened and she nibbled my hands with her teeth. This made me smile and feel grateful cause I never thought I'd live to see the day. Later Mantee swam off and beached herself on a riverbank, squirming to get some marsh grass. I followed and rolled in the mud til we were covered in the stuff, declaring, "This is the best." After that, we locked back in and Mantee was never far away.

I returned to work that afternoon with a hop in my step. The Cap'n had me serving drinks for a card game that took place in the STATE ROOM. As I poured soda into fancy glasses, I realized these people were a family of some sort and real gamblers. In fact, it wasn't long til they challenged me to a game of blackjack. Now, I been around the block a few times so I didn't tell 'em that when it comes to games, I'm the champ.

"You in for a round?" asked the Cap'n.

"No doubt," I answered.

"We're gonna have some fun!"

And that's how it began. I played all kinds of games that week: poker, roulette, even ones I never knew like gin, spades, and rummy. But when the stakes got too high, I'd always say goodnight, cause I knew if I went on a bad run, I'd get cleaned out for sure. In fact, I was down to my last pennies and had nuthin' left but the clothes on my back.

"You low on cash?" asked the Cap'n.

"I'm alright," I answered.

"No kidding," were the words I heard as I slipped away from the tables and went outside. Despite having nothing to my name, the air brightened my mood and I went to sleep that night believing all things were possible.

In this way we twisted through North Cralina, each day bringin' a new town: 'Lizbeth City, Bo-fert, Southport. Mantee stuck behind us like glue and I showed Half-Pint everything there was to know about sea cows. We'd hang our legs off the back of *Lady Luck* and I'd explain how mantees float through the water and suck up seagrass like vacuums. "Seaweed," I'd say, "yum," and pop some in my mouth.

"I'm not eatin' that," declared Half-Pint, but it didn't take long til we were both chewin' it down like real mantees and I realized: that's why I like kids, they're not scared like adults. In fact, I told Half-Pint, "Never grow up, grow down."

"Grow down?" wondered Half-Pint.

"Yeah," I replied and it was at that moment I first noticed palm trees in the distance. The tidal currents had carried us through many inlets and as *Lady Luck* fell in line with other boats shuffling toward Myrtle Beach, I knew this chapter was comin' to a close. I think everyone else sensed it too cause as we sailed into a marina they called a big game for that night.

"The Cap'n is a serious gambler," warned Junior and I nodded in agreement cause I knew it to be true. Later, when Half-Pint and I were leading Mantee to a cove far from all the nasty boats, a plan popped into my head. A plan so secret I wasn't sure I should tell anyone, but then I figured, I could whisper anything in the world to Half-Pint and it would be safe cause no one believes lil' kids anyway. So I did.

"Whoa," exclaimed Half-Pint.

"Yeah." I replied and we talked about things til the sun set below the horizon.

Five card draw. That's the game the Cap'n wanted to play. It's a simple game where hands have names like full house, straight, and flush. Being a big-time gambler, the Cap'n would have an advantage, but as long as I followed my gut, I could beat anyone. Thoughts like this filled my mind as I entered the STATE ROOM that night. The tables were filling up and cards were spread face down. I saw the Cap'n leaning against a wooden beam, smiling. We took our seats and the game began.

"Ante up," said the dealer and everyone tossed dollars into a pot with anticipation. The cards were dealt out and before I knew it, the Cap'n won the first hand. My pockets were empty so I covered the bet with the only thing I had left: my medal of St. Christopher.

The game continued. I won some and lost some. Bets were placed and people came and went til there was no one left but the Cap'n and me.

"One last hand?" asked the Cap'n.

"I'm in," I replied.

"What's your wager?"

Silence hung over the table. I knew from getting hustled in NYC that it's a mistake to rely on small-time bets; play big and high.

"I bet three months of work on *Lady Luck* against the sailboat you got tied out back." I replied.

Eyebrows were raised and I could see the Cap'n staring straight at me.

"Deal."

The final game began.

Cards were dealt quickly and I picked up my hand. A couple of face cards, but nothing great. A sinking feeling began forming in the pit of my stomach and I felt sweat on my palms. The Cap'n discarded casually but my eyes caught a tiny shift in posture and something about that movement gave me hope.

The game continued.

I received three new cards. My face was expressionless and everyone sensed tension in the room.

"Whatcha got?" I asked.

"Four of a kind," the Cap'n replied, laying four cards onto the table with a smirk. It was a powerful hand that's hard to beat. "You?"

I took a deep breath and cleared my mind. It's hard to describe what happened next, but I felt invisible forces gather all around me, from Junior, Half-Pint, the hull of Lady Luck, the waves, the beaches, even the moon itself.

The cards were revealed: Ten. Jack. Queen. King. Ace.

A royal flush.

I won.

The crowd jumped with surprise. The Cap'n banged the table but then took a deep breath and walked over toward me, saying, "That's somethin' else."

"Beginners luck," I exhaled and for the remainder of the evening, people kept shaking my hands and giving me hugs. Half-Pint was the nicest of all and said, "Happy day!"

That's the story of how I lucked into a sailboat. After the fuss of the game was over I found myself back in the cove with Mantee, swimmin' under the moon. Mantee is graceful for such a large creature and as we twirled through the water it dawned on me what's so special about life. Parents and teachers may tell you otherwise, but happiness doesn't come from good grades or a job or anything like that, it comes from being wild and free.

No one dares tell you this but it's true.

CHAPTER 9

SLEEPING GIANT

I HUNG around Myrtle Beach for a few more days. The town was full of people and shops but I didn't care about that stuff, I needed to learn how to sail my new boat. The thing had no motor and used wind for power, so it was hard to control. In fact, I crashed twice in the harbor til Junior and Tully taught me things like tacking and how to trim a mainsail. After that, I was cruisin' like a champ and could feel the pull of adventure calling me back.

The next morning I said my goodbyes to the Cap'n and everyone on *Lady Luck*.

"I owe you my life," I told 'em.

"You don't owe us anything but a thank you and a goodbye," replied the Cap'n, so that's what I gave. Half-Pint was cryin' so I stayed a while longer and told jokes til we laughed. I knew the kid would grow up to be a great person and as I sailed away, I named my new boat *God's Gift* in honor of the lil' nipper. Then I set a course back to Mantee and away we went.

"Ay yo!" I yelled as wind filled the sails and we cut across rivers and bays. This may sound easy, but truth be told, *God's Gift* was a tough boat. When the air was calm we'd be dead in the water, but if a gust picked up, the mast would swing round and nearly take off my head. When that happened, I'd duck down and watch the shoreline speed by. Mantee (bless her heart) would always stay close to the boat. With her broad tail she looked like a mermaid and it was around this time I noticed algae growin' on her back.

"No way," I declared, jumping in to get a closer look. Sure enough, there were green patches everywhere and I rubbed in amazement. Do you know what Mantee's skin feels like? Imagine an elephant, wrinkled but firm, or your arm when it has goosebumps or a balloon that's overfilled. It's a mystery why algae appeared and Mantee scraped every dock we passed trying to get it off, but she was grassy now and that's how it would be.

After that, the weather cooled and we slowed down. The days were getting shorter and Mantee was taking frequent naps. One moment we'd be drifting along, the next she'd be crash-landing onto the bottom for a rest. When that happened, she'd hang motionless in the water, come up for air, then back down to snooze. Up. Down. Up. Down. The whole thing had me restless but I soon realized Mantee was teaching me patience. I had to respect her wish to sleep and not get in the way. Time passed and there was nothing to do so I observed little things.

For instance, Mantee's eyesight is bad. I know this cause she detects me by feel rather than sight. Also, Mantee has fingernails. They're at the end of her flippers and look like lil' peanuts. And did you know Mantee can't turn her head? If she wants to look around then her whole body spins like a ship turning in the ocean. There are things I'm leaving out, but this will help you understand what I learned about Mantee while she slept.

More time passed.

At some point my food ran out and I burned with hunger. Wild boars appeared on the shore and my belly growled. They were real razorbacks and I thought about trapping 'em for food, but couldn't do it. I got no stomach for guttin' piggies, so seaweed would have to do. Lucky for us the rivers in South Cralina are full of veggies and we ate our way through gardens of stuff til we came upon the city of Charleston.

Imagine living in a pretty town by the sea. As I climbed outta my boat and walked past fancy homes I pictured myself a big shot. In reality, I was a bag of bones.

When you're hungry and there's little to eat, even insects look delicious. A bug flew by and I snatched it out of the air, but couldn't gulp it down. What I really wanted was a hot meal so I wandered the city looking for work.

Before long, I found a job cuttin' grass for rich people. It was tough pushing a lawn mower all day but soon there was enough money to last for weeks. I ran back to the harbor to tell Mantee the good news, but stopped with surprise. A crowd of gangsters had gathered on the seawall and were chuckin' stones into the water.

"Hey, watch where you're throwin'!" I yelled.

"What's it to you?" they asked.

"Someone's out there," I shouted. Sure enough, Mantee was sleeping by the shallow bank. One of the gangsters lined up a shot and blasted her in the back with a stone. I trembled with anger but remembered it's important to control yourself, so I shut my eyes and counted to ten. Then I took a deep breath and said, "You oughta go home."

"Forget it, we're just having fun," they laughed and took off someplace else. Maybe these gangsters were beautiful to their families, but they were ugly to me. At least that's what I thought til Mantee popped up and took a deep breath: whoosh; then back down. The sound of that big ol' breath made me calm and I thought,

"That's all there is to it." I mean, I could complain, but why?

After that, the weather warmed so we left with the tides. Mantee was awake now and full of energy. Her tail moved up and down and we cut across wide stretches of water. Occasionally fishing boats would pass by, checking us out.

"What's that thing?" they'd shout.

"A mantee," I'd reply.

"No kidding."

CHAPTER 10

FIRE ON HORSE ISLAND

I DON'T KNOW how long we'd been gone, but if I kept a diary I would've written, "Already October?" It seemed so long ago that we left NYC. A gentle breeze filled the sail and I cruised near the shore to try and spot wildlife. All kinds of critters appeared and I renamed everything I saw: pelicans became pellies; rabbits were scrabbits; even bumblebees were grumblebees. I do this cause it makes the world seem less ordinary.

That night we made camp at the mouth of a marshy creek. Mantee grazed while I searched for solid ground. Soon enough I found a path in the woods that led to an old cabin. No one was home, so I went inside and looked into a mirror for the first time in months. I almost didn't recognize the face that looked back! It wasn't that I was starved from all the hunger, it was the way I stared that seemed older somehow. I could've looked into the mirror for hours but had to turn away, it was too weird.

The next morning we left before sunrise. Mantee floated like a stick in the water while I tried to keep up. At some point we passed into Mother Georgia and that's where the rivers started twistin' like snakes. I struggled to steer through the winding channels and kept crashing into mud banks. After a while I jumped out and pulled *God's Gift* by the prow. For miles I dragged the thing through shallow marshes. People on the land would watch and laugh.

"You spring a leak?" they'd shout.

"Sumptin' like that," I'd answer, too proud to admit I was a beginner.

Finally the river widened and emptied into the sea.

"This way, Mantee!" I yelled, climbing back into the boat. Our course was due south and we moved down the coast til a big island came into view. It was surrounded on all sides by high surf and when I saw that wild water, I wanted to stay away, but Mantee kept going, so I followed. The current was fierce and *God's Gift* started rippin' toward the distant shore. It wasn't long til I lost control of the boat.

"Watch out!" I shouted as *God's Gift* shipwrecked onto the island. The rudder snapped and I flew forward into the sand. The pain was incredible. For a few seconds

I lay on the beach looking at swaying palm trees. Then everything went dark.

When I woke up a horse was lickin' my face.

"Hold on," I mumbled, blinking in surprise. It really was a horse. The face and mane were unmistakable. I closed my eyes and thought, *this isn't real, I'm dreaming*, but when I opened my eyes I saw four more of 'em. They stomped the ground and snorted. I lay still and they trotted over to a patch of grass.

I sat up.

My back hurt but I couldn't take my eyes off these horses. One of 'em had a shaggy head so I named it CC like yours truly. The others I named Doc, Blaze, Raisin, and Scamp. I could tell they were wild cause they roamed the beach without a care in the world. Finally they disappeared into the dunes.

I got onto my feet.

The first thing I noticed was *God's Gift* smashed to pieces. I thought I'd sail that boat til the end, but here I was, stranded again. It was low tide and Mantee appeared near the water's edge. I waded into the surf and Mantee swam over to nibble my foot. Then she took a deep breath and dove back down to hunt for food. I stood still and tried to gather myself.

How was I gonna get off this island?

Whatever the answer, I couldn't sleep that night. My

food was gone and I woke up thirsty. Before long, I went looking for the horses, they would know where to find fresh water. Sure enough, I found 'em drinking from a hidden spring. I crawled over and took a big gulp of water. It tasted great. The horses neighed and searched my clothes for food. "I got nuthin'," I laughed. One of 'em bent down and dripped water onto my head. "Now you did it," I exclaimed. After that, we became friends and I stayed near the horses to try and survive.

I found out there were four parts to a horse's day: grazing, drinking, playing and fighting. Grazing was my favorite cause I would hunt for berries while they munched on dune grass. Eventually the berries ran out and I ate rose petals. When the roses ran out, I ate snails. It got worse and worse til I stumbled into the water looking for anybody. A person? A boat? Mantee?

There was no one.

The world being what it is, I started to suffer.

Back at the spring I tried to drink but everything tasted different. I couldn't sleep. At one point I jumped onto a horse's back and galloped down the beach before being thrown into the waves.

"Mantee, where are you?" I moaned.

I closed my eyes and felt sick.

Nighttime was the worst of all. I would roam up and down the island til I was shaking and sweaty. If I could only sleep for a few hours my mind would be okay, but thunder boomed in the distance and I knew there'd be no rest.

Then the wind started to roar. Like a fool I stood on the beach and stared at the incoming storm. Lightning danced across the sky and hit the island in an instant. I ducked down and counted six strikes. The nasty bolts must've hit dead trees and underbrush cause everything burst into flames. Fire swept the island and I ran for my life.

The blaze was fierce. I tried to get away but stumbled and fell onto my face. What happened next is a blur. I remember hooves pounding on the sand. Thunder cracked and the horses reared up on their hind legs. Lightning flashed and made their shadows look terrifying. For the first time in my life I shouted, "O God!" Smoke filled my lungs and I collapsed onto the ground. I was finished, that's what it looked like.

CHAPTER 11

PAPA MANTEE

BUT I DIDN'T DIE.

The Lord takes care of those who never give up. I was about to take my last breath when the clouds parted and moonlight flashed down on the water. That's when I saw something large out in the waves. At first I thought it was Mantee, but it was too different, too chunky. I knew it had to be a Papa Mantee.

What's a Papa Mantee?

A Papa Mantee is a sea cow that appears in time to give you hope. When I saw its big body through the smoke and flames, everything became clear. We were no longer lost. Out in that water was a new friend and soon there would be hundreds more; maybe thousands. Then courage came to me and I was okay again. All the torture on the beach was a memory. I got up and ran into the surf, leaping and yelling. In fact, it was my greatest leap and loudest shout of "Ay yo!" After that, the fire dimmed. Stars came out and the Papa Mantee floated near my legs.

"Lookit what we got here," I marveled.

The Papa Mantee chuffed and rolled over. I could see a dark spot on its belly and realized it was a belly button. What a discovery! My eyes took in every detail cause I wanted to tell Mantee about this sweet creature. With only its tail moving, the Papa Mantee swayed side to side and lifted its nostrils into the air.

"Where you from?" I wondered.

If the Papa Mantee could talk it might've said, "Heaven."

Instead, the Papa Mantee munched on seagrass, its big teeth going chomp chomp. The sound was comforting so I made a little prayer. "Please bless all living things." The prayer made me feel good and I waved goodbye as the Papa Mantee disappeared into the night.

The next day I couldn't stop smiling. Even though the island was torched and the horses covered in ash, we were happy to be alive, one way or another.

Meanwhile, the storm had washed over the entire island and left piles of junk on the beach. There were toothbrushes, books, even a can of beans. But the best thing I found was an ol' canoe. It looked like a wreck and was covered in barnacles, but the thing could float. On top of that, there was a fishing pole tied to the stern. I couldn't believe my luck and named it *Spanish Galleon* cause it was like treasure to me. I slipped the *Galleon* into the water and a mess of fish appeared which I caught and roasted over a fire til they were nice and delicious.

By noon I saw with relief the familiar shape of Mantee close to shore. I dove into the tide and started talkin' to her excitedly. I can't remember the exact words, but I said things like:

"Say, where you been?"

"Another mantee was here, you shoulda seen it ."

"I wonder how many mantees are out there? Must be a couple hundred for sure."

"We gotta find more of 'em, you know?"

But Mantee didn't answer. Instead, she swam around and made big circles in the water, like she was trying to communicate. What it actually meant, only Mantee knows for sure, but it was probably something like, "Lessgo." So that's what we did.

We left Horse Island the next morning and headed for the Sunshine State. At first I had trouble steering the *Galleon* in the open sea. I'd push an oar into the water and spin left, then right, but soon enough I was rowing in a straight course. The wind blasted through my hair and the horizon seemed endless.

Steadily we kept on.

Hours passed.

At some point we entered a bay that was stacked with boats. Some were tied to docks while others raced around like maniacs. Mantee and I stayed far from the crowds and found a quiet cove to take a rest. When the sun got red, I waded into the water to say goodnight. Mantee swam over and I held out my arms. For the first time EVER she gave me a hug. I couldn't believe it. Mantee's snout pressed into my belly and her flippers grabbed my waist. It lasted only a moment, but when I looked into those button-shaped eyes, it made me laugh out loud. Then Mantee floated away and fell asleep.

I smiled and wondered: you ever feel bad in life and then realize, what difference does it make? That's what I was thinkin' as some teenagers started a bonfire on a distant beach and when they set off firecrackers, everyone cheered.

Then there was perfect stillness.

CHAPTER 12

FLURDA

You started at the beginning and now you're almost at the end; that's wild. I usually don't read books, it's better to be outside, always. So why did I write these words? Cause I want you to know how the story goes. At some point we passed into Flurda and saw our first pastel sunset. Bright colors melted into tropical water and I liked the place straight away.

Morning came and we started off at a booming pace. There were miles of winding rivers and I rowed next to Mantee, making sure to take occasional breaks cause if my arms got tired then it would be goodbye forever. Eventually we came to a swamp that was full of mangroves that were like giant trees growing out of the water. Mantee floated between the roots and ate leaves right off the branches. I climbed the trunk of a big mangrove to look around and in every direction were lizards, snakes, even a nasty gator. I got nervous when the gator swam toward us, but Mantee nudged it aside like an old log and I knew things would be okay. When the gator looked my way, I shook my fist in the air and yelled, "Bah!" Then I laughed and gave a new name to everything in sight: Professor Palmtree, Speedy the Turtle, Grand Goose, and so on.

The reason I'm tellin' you all this is cause that's when a whole new set of adventures got goin'.

We wandered along many shores.

I fished as often as I could.

I developed a knack for cookin' fishies over a fire. I'd sit and nibble at the meat til there was a warm buzz all over my body.

One time, Mantee and I found a hidden bayou with reefs that stuck out of the water at low tide. Every morning some racoons would come rustlin' through the marsh grass and cause the fish to jump outta the water and make a terrific splash. It was the funniest little drama that ever took place.

Heck, each day was a new discovery.

At St. Augustine we floated under railway arches and when a train went by the whole river shook and flowed backwards.

Another time, we passed a flock of birds on a sandbar

and when we got close to 'em they rose into the air and made the sky dark as night.

Through it all we were blessed with a will that made our hearts keep going.

Of course, we didn't count these adventures as the end of our story. Rather, they were small parts of a thousand things that can never be forgotten. So we laughed and joked and time slipped by til the day came when we had to say goodbye. I can't remember every detail about those last hours with Mantee, but I'm gonna give it a try. Here goes.

The day was warm like so many others. After crossing the mouth of a river we found ourselves in a hidden pool that sparkled in the Flurda sun. Wild bananas grew near the shore so I called the place Banana Lagoon. It was late afternoon. Mantee and I drifted through the clear spring when something caught my eye cause I started lookin' everywhere for signs of life and sure enough, that's what I found.

A gray face popped up out of the water with long whiskers, two eyes and a couple of nose holes. Then another. And another.

I nearly fell over when I realized we were surrounded by mantees.

You shoulda seen 'em, they were super-sized. Some were big as rowboats, others were like giant swimming potatoes. One must've been a thousand pounds or more. They'd take deep breaths and dive to the bottom, leaving swirly patterns on the surface of the water. That's how I knew there were so many of 'em.

"Mantee," I gasped, wanting to get her attention, but she didn't need any introductions. All the mantees had gathered round us and wanted to make friends. They touched faces and talked in squeaks underwater. Mantee rolled onto her back and I could tell she was showing off. Soon others rolled on their backs and joined in the fun. For a moment I think I experienced what it's like to be a mantee, so connected with each other and the surroundings.

After that, Mantee went off, swimming and playing with the others. As I watched her disappear, a feeling of relief washed over me. It's hard to believe we traveled all the way down the east coast and survived for so long. "O Mantee," I thought, "this will be your home." When I went to sleep that night I couldn't help but smile.

The next morning I got up and took a tour of Banana Lagoon. The place was full of mantees and I gave 'em all names like Meatus Loaf, Full Quart, and Grumpus. In the afternoon I found some newborn calves with stubby round faces. I named one of these Baby Snoot but later changed it to Lil' Snoot cause it wouldn't stay a baby for long. Lil' Snoot swam next to its mom and this allowed me to see far into the future: Mantee would be a mother and be so happy. It was that simple.

I stayed for a while longer, but at some point I said, "This is it."

Before I left Banana Lagoon, I took one last swim.

As I floated through the herd, a splendid realization entered my head. Mantees are our dreams. If you neglect them, they become cold and die. But if you put your whole self into them and never give up, they make it to warm water. Have you ever floated in a warm pool of water with the sun shining on your face? It feels amazing.

I can't explain it, I'm just excited by life.